Dedication

To Margaret Tanner, my very dear friend and fellow author, for her enduring encouragement and friendship.

To Alan, my husband of over forty-nine years, who has been a relentless supporter of my writing and dreams for many years.

To You, my wonderful readers, who encourage me to continue writing these stories. It is such a joy knowing so many of you enjoy reading my stories as much as I love writing them for you.

Table of Contents

Chapter One

Clutching her carpetbag tightly, Victoria Hudson leaned back, then closing her eyes, hoped the long ride would soon be over.

When she set out to become a teacher, she hadn't envisaged traveling this far from home. Especially with the promise of only one year at most with each contract she accepted.

Teaching positions were hard to find, particularly if you happened to be female. She grimaced at the thought.

Her eyes fluttered open as she heard chuckling.

"Were you laughing at me," she asked boldly. She didn't know this stranger sitting opposite her, and never would. They would go their separate ways along the line, and never lay eyes on each other again.

He chuckled again. "I was." He grinned, not even trying to hide his actions. "I've been watching you, studying your pretty face."

She felt the heat creep up her neck and cheeks.

"Then suddenly you pulled the most gruesome face." This time his laughter was less contained.

Victoria harrumphed. "You are very rude, Mr..."

"Pendleberry. Jesse Pendleberry, and I don't think I'm the least bit rude. I'm being honest about the situation."

She studied him. The man was well-dressed, she couldn't deny that, but his chin was covered with dark stubble and his eyes were red.

Her hands flew to her own face. Were her eyes red from lack of sleep? She didn't want to make a bad first impression when she arrived in Grand Falls. Oh, and goodness only knew what sort of mess her hair was in. At least she could cover it with her bonnet once she alighted the train.

She continued to stare, not wanting to add to this bizarre conversation, but the silence finally got to her. "Well Mr Pendleberry, I think you *were* being rude. A gentleman..."

He tried to stifle another chuckle, but didn't quite succeed. "Who says I'm a gentleman, Mrs...?" He paused and she glared at him.

"I am not married," she blurted out, then wanted to take back her words but it was too late. She did not know this man, and had no idea what he was capable of. "I am *Miss* Victoria Hudson." She pursed her lips as she studied him further, then suddenly relaxed them. Mother always told her it made her look like a matronly old maid when she did that.

Besides, it encouraged wrinkles, Mother said it did. She certainly did not want wrinkles at the age of twenty-four.

She watched as he glanced at her left hand. Did he not believe her? The cheek of the man! "Mr Pendleberry," she said gruffly, "My marital status is none of your business!" She hoped her level of indignation came through loud and clear.

He grinned again, but this time she noticed the dimples that sat either side of his beautifully formed lips. "I beg to differ, Miss Hudson," he said, continuing to grin.

Was he trying to goad her now?

"I might like to spend more time with you. After all, you are the most beautiful woman I've seen for a very long time."

She smiled, but suddenly pulled herself into line. This man could be the worst of the worst. The type of person her mother had warned her about.

Victoria began to stand, straightening her skirts as she did so. She clutched her carpetbag even tighter to her chest, having decided to take a short stroll along the corridor to stretch her legs. Also to get away from the captivating man sitting opposite.

Mr Pendleberry also stood. Did he intend to follow her? Her heart began to beat hard, making her feel light-headed.

The train jerked to a stop and she fell...right into Mr Pendleberry's arms.

Jesse looked down. He couldn't believe his luck.

It wasn't often beautiful women fell at your feet. Well, okay, she hadn't fallen at his feet, but she did fall right into his arms.

And what a woman she was.

Miss Victoria Hudson was beautiful, and it was all he could do not to reach out and brush his fingers down her cheeks. And her hair – it was golden brown and wayward strands ran loose down her back. Restraint was called for right now, but he didn't have a lot of it.

He stared at her – her eyes were wide open in shock. His arms had crept around her in an effort to stop her falling. He'd certainly achieved that.

She scowled at him. "You can let me go now." She looked annoyed. *Was it his fault the train suddenly jerked to a stop?*

They weren't at their destination. A glance out the window told him that much. Most likely a group of cows had straddled the tracks.

He sighed. This was a long enough trip without it being longer. But on the bright side, Miss Hudson's company made it bearable.

He grinned.

"What's so funny," she asked gruffly. "Not me, I hope." She scowled again. He didn't like it when she scowled. She was far prettier when she smiled.

"I was just thinking about the odds of such a beauty landing in the arms of the likes of me."

She pulled out of his arms and straightened up. "I guess I should thank you for saving me." He glanced down as she tried to straighten the creases out of her skirts. But it was far too late for that.

He gave a little mock bow. "You are very welcome, Miss Hudson."

She grinned and began to walk away. He followed her, since he had previously intended to stretch his legs.

She glanced back over her shoulder, then turned to the front again. They hadn't gone far when the whistle of the train blew and the train jerked for a second time.

The alluring Miss Hudson was thrown into his arms again. "We have to stop meeting like this," he said. He laughed but she did not.

"Blasted trains," she huffed, then took off down the corridor. He stood staring after her.

Victoria returned to her seat and waited, but Mr Pendleberry did not return. She wondered where he had gone.

The protocol was to return to your allocated seat once you'd sat there, and most people abided by the rule.

Not Mr Pendleberry apparently – he was nowhere in sight. She worried he was hurt somewhere.

She stared out the soot-covered window. They surely must be arriving soon. She'd been on this rickety contraption for days now.

She hated trains. Despised them even more than the stage coach. She'd endured both over the past few years when attending her various posts.

She really wished women were offered the same teaching conditions as men. So far, none of her teaching appointments had lasted more than six months. In the majority of cases, she was deemed a visiting teacher, filling in until a male teacher could be found.

It really irked her.

"Grand Falls, Grand Falls." The conductor glanced down at her. "Grand Falls is the next stop, Miss," he said. "You can collect your luggage on the main platform."

"Thank you," she said, and handed him a gold coin. He'd been most helpful during the long trip, and she greatly appreciated it. "Oh," she said suddenly. "Do you know if Mr Pendleberry is alright? I haven't seen him for awhile."

He nodded. "He's safely tucked up in the next carriage, Miss. Got talking to a gent up there." He moved away before she could ask him anything more.

She hadn't thought about it much before, but now wondered where he was heading. She had no idea about this man who had caught her attention, and now she never would.

If she was truthful with herself, Victoria had enjoyed being held in his arms. Had enjoyed their short chatter, and had most certainly enjoyed looking at him.

Jesse Pendleberry was a ruggedly handsome young man, especially with the whiskers currently showing on his chin.

The train whistle blew, and she waited on her seat for the train to stop. She was not going to risk being thrown about again. There was plenty of time since the train was scheduled to stop here at Grand Falls for twenty minutes before proceeding to the next town.

She played with her hair and pulled it into a chignon, then tucked it up into her bonnet, which she fastened under her chin. Victoria hated to think what she looked like – she was sure to be a complete and utter mess.

Why did she agree to travel so far from home? She was more than happy in Buffalo, Wyoming, but admittedly, the work for a lady teacher simply wasn't there.

She took a deep breath. Victoria had been over this scenario so many times before. Her life would be so much different had she been born male. But she hadn't, and she had to accept the fact.

As the train jerked to a halt, despite her best efforts she was thrown from her seat again. She landed on the floor this time, since the elusive Mr Pendleberry was nowhere to be seen.

The conductor came scurrying to her aid, helping her back onto her seat. Victoria wondered would he have been so helpful had she not lined his hand with a gold coin.

Stop it, Victoria! she told herself. *That is just horrid.*

She looked up into his face. "Thank you. I appreciate it," she said as he helped her back onto her seat.

"Oh my dear Miss Hudson!" It was her former traveling companion this time. "I do apologize. I should have stayed and ensured your safety."

She glared at him. "I am not your responsibility," she said gruffly, then watched as he shook his head, and sat opposite her.

Why did men think they could rule over women? She'd only known this man a day or two at most. She'd totally lost track of time and had no idea when, or even where, he'd boarded.

"It was nice meeting you," she said equally as gruffly, then still clutching her carpetbag, left the carriage.

Jesse stood on the platform checking his supplies. He'd brought several large boxes with him, and once settled, would make additional orders as necessary.

The trip had been made more pleasant by the company of the charming Miss Hudson, but he'd probably never see her again.

She'd stormed off in a huff after the train had completely stopped, most likely moved to another carriage far from where she'd originally sat. Far away from him.

For some reason she'd taken a dislike to him. He shrugged his shoulders – there was nothing he could do about it even though he wished he could.

As he went through the manifest, he worried about the contents. Many items were made of glass, and trains were so unpredictable, and as he'd seen first-hand, often unsteady. He hoped none had smashed on the journey.

Grand Falls was the last place he'd had in mind for his new venture, but it was fast-growing, and his research had shown it to have a lot of prospects for his type of business.

It was also fairly isolated, which meant customers would not have other local options. Yes, this was a good decision.

At least he hoped it was.

"Mr Pendleberry?" He glanced up. The porter stared at him.

"Sorry, I was deep in thought." He signed the manifest and handed it over. "Can you arrange delivery for me? In say, an hour? That would give me enough time to get settled and ready for all of this to arrive." He waved his hands across the boxes before him.

Jesse reached into his pocket and pulled out a wad of notes, handing one over. The porter stared in disbelief.

"Of course, Mr Pendleberry." He continued to stare at the crumpled two-dollar note in his hand. "I'll make sure this lot is safely stored until then."

"I appreciate it," Jesse said as he walked away. "Those boxes are very fragile." Now to collect his luggage.

He strolled away from the area dedicated to commercial goods, and headed toward the main platform. His heart skipped a beat as he spotted Miss Hudson awaiting her luggage.

He sidled up beside her. "Nice to see you again."

She spun around to face him, her hand to her chest. "Oh! You surprised me." Then she scowled. "What are you doing here?"

Did she think she was the only one allowed to alight at Grand Falls? "What are you doing here?" he countered, only he was grinning.

Things just got interesting.

"I'm the new…" She suddenly stopped. "I'm new to Grand Falls," she said gruffly, as though she'd accidentally told him her darkest secret.

Two could play at that game. "Ah," he said, but declined to offer further information. Perhaps because he knew it would irritate her?

A different porter arrived with her luggage. "Here you are, Miss Hudson." He pushed the trolley toward her. "You're not going to be able to carry this one," he said, pointing to the larger of the two valises.

"I have luggage to collect too," Jesse said, handing over his ticket. He leaned in to pick up her luggage. "My Lord," he said. "What on earth is in that largest valise?"

She glared at him. "That's for me to know and you to find out."

He liked Miss Victoria Hudson, she was fun. She might not realize it, but she was. He was enjoying their game of cat and mouse.

For the time being anyway.

His luggage arrived and was placed on the same trolley. "How much will it cost to have this lot delivered?"

The porter thought about it momentarily. "One dollar for the four cases."

Jesse nodded his acceptance. "What's your address? I can carry mine from there."

Her eyes opened wide. "I'm not…"

He predicted her answer before she'd even opened her mouth.

"Miss Hudson?" The voice was loud and clear. "Miss Victoria Hudson?"

The woman was older and looked very respectable. Trustworthy. Jesse turned to study her. "Your aunt?" he asked.

Miss Hudson scurried to her. "Mrs Baker? Oh thank you for coming to collect me."

Jesse stepped forward. "Mrs Baker," he said, extending his hand. "I am Jesse Pendleberry, the new apothecarist for Grand Falls."

She looked him up and down, then accepted his proffered hand. Then a slow smile came to her face. "We're getting an apothecary? Oh my goodness. That is wonderful news!"

"I have just offered to have Miss Hudson's luggage delivered along with mine to wherever she is staying. I can carry mine from there, but hers is far too heavy to carry."

"Really?" The older woman stared at Miss Hudson questioningly.

"School books," she said quietly.

Why couldn't she have told *him* that? The woman was simply being difficult. He'd already determined she didn't like him, and despite that, he still was trying to help her out.

She was beginning to grate on him.

Mrs Baker turned to Jesse. "Delivery to the church hall would be far better. That's where classes will be held."

Ah, Miss Hudson was the new schoolmarm. Who would have guessed?

He turned to the porter who had been waiting patiently for a resolution. "Here's a dollar," he said as the man's eyes widened. "Do you know where the church hall is?"

"I sure do," he said, then took off with the trolley full of luggage and a spring in his step.

Chapter Two

Jesse whistled all the way from the church hall to his store.

He'd had a rather pleasant trip, despite the continued jostling he'd endured. Miss Victoria Hudson was a breath of fresh air, even if she did give him a hard time.

The thought made him grin. She was rather feisty, which made her entertaining. He'd never in his life refused the offer of enjoyment.

The look on her face when she'd discovered he'd disembarked at Grand Falls was a sight to behold. He wondered how long she would stay here.

The same question applied to himself. If his business was not fruitful, he would have to move on, despite the expense he'd gone to before he'd even set up shop.

The store itself had sat empty for some years, and he'd bought it sight unseen. Albeit at a rather discounted price. Rather than pay board elsewhere, he'd had the local carpenter make adjustments to include a small residence at the back.

It wasn't uncommon, he'd been told, as several other store owners had a residence at the rear too. Since it was only him, and he had no plan to marry anytime this decade, let alone the near future, it would suit him perfectly.

So why did Miss Hudson enter his mind? Jesse shook himself. It was time to get his mind on business and set up shop. Most of all, he needed to vanquish the new schoolmarm to the deepest depths of his mind.

He dropped his luggage to the ground and unlocked the door to the residence. He found the bedroom and put his luggage aside, then did a quick walk through. Not that there was much to see. He'd asked Patrick Harper to build a fully furnished residence that included a bedroom, sitting room, kitchen and bathroom. That was exactly what he got.

Jesse ran his hands over the doorframes. The craftmanship was excellent. He couldn't fault any of the work.

He walked through to his new store via the lockable adjoining door and checked the layout. It was exactly the way he'd requested. Soon his delivery would arrive, and he'd be busy for the rest of the day.

Tomorrow he would open the doors and wait for the customers to come. For a town that had never had an apothecary, it will be interesting to see what sort of response he got. If Mrs Baker's reaction was an indication, his day could be quite busy.

Jesse stood back and envisioned his new store. He'd spent many years training for this under the best apothecarist – his Uncle Joshua.

After he'd died suddenly the store was sold from under him. Jesse would have paid a reasonable price, but his cousin Samson hiked up the price so far, it was out of reach.

Samson had been lazy from early childhood, and despite his father's attempts to teach him, refused to learn the trade. Wanting to pass the family business on, he'd taught Jesse all he knew. The pity of it was his uncle had not allowed for it in his will.

After all, one never expected to be trampled by horses pulling a runaway wagon, especially at such a young age.

He sighed. Jesse really missed his uncle. After his parents had died in a stage coach accident, he'd taken Jesse in. Samson had despised him ever since, vowing to get back at him one day. He was true to his word.

The knock at the door brought him out of his dark thoughts. He smiled as he opened the door. It was time to set up his shop.

"Oh, this is lovely, Mrs Baker. Thank you for accommodating me."

The other woman beamed. "I'm happy to have you, my dear. I'm used to putting up strays. There is one condition though…"

Victoria's heart thudded. What was she expected to do in exchange for her lodgings? "Of course I'm willing to pay."

Mrs Baker waved her concerns aside. "I'm more than happy for you to stay here for as long as it takes. No payment necessary."

Her heart pounded. It was worse than she originally thought.

She swallowed… hard.

"I…"

Mrs Baker stepped toward her and held her hands. "My dear girl, I didn't mean to scare you! No, my condition is very simple. Allow me to teach you to cook."

Victoria's heart settled down and she felt suddenly better.

"Young women these days are useless in the kitchen. Our men need someone who can cook for them." She quirked an eyebrow at Victoria. "Or can you cook already?"

"No, no I can't," she said quickly. "There are no plans to marry either."

She stepped back at the astonished expression that met her words. "Not marry? My goodness." She snatched up a newspaper from the table and began to fan herself. "Your generation rebel far too much against convention." She slipped onto a chair and stared at Victoria.

"I... I have aspirations," she said firmly. "I have wanted to teach school since I was ten." She squared her shoulders and stared back. "The rules of teaching state once a woman marries she can no longer teach."

She pursed her lips in defiance, then recalled her mother's harsh words. She shrugged her shoulders into relaxing, then relaxed her whole face. "I decided long ago not to marry."

A slight smile curved the lips of her hostess. "That very well may change." She fanned her face again, then put down the newspaper. "That Mr Pendleberry – he's taken a liking to you." This time she grinned.

Victoria frowned. "He is so infuriating, and I don't like him one little bit." That caused Mrs Baker to laugh out loud.

"Oh, so you really like him then?"

Her eyes opened wide at the woman's words. "I most certainly do not." She flicked her skirts as though that put an end to the discussion. "Now Mrs Baker, would you like me to put the kettle on for a nice cup of tea?"

The day had finally come.

Today was to be the first day of school. Mrs Baker warned her not to expect too much. Many of the parents wouldn't allow their children to attend school as they were needed to help out. The majority would be coming from out of town, and lived on ranches where they were required to assist with the daily chores.

She felt disheartened, but knew there was a possibility Mrs Baker was wrong.

At least she hoped she was.

Victoria made her bed and dressed. She pulled her long hair into a chignon and would place a bonnet on her head before she made her way to the makeshift school. She'd already set up the chairs the day before.

Proper desks would be far better, but what choice did she have? She had to work with what she was given. Luckily she had brought some supplies with her. She'd been caught out before with these small town schools, and wasn't willing to be unprepared again.

She sat opposite Mrs Baker in the large kitchen and sipped her tea. "What are they like?" she asked, glancing across at her most generous hostess.

"The children?" She laughed. "That wholly depends on who turns up today." She put down her newspaper and applied all her attention to Victoria.

"I doubt Johnny Ambrewster will be there. He's one of the older children and his father will likely keep him home."

Victoria stiffened. She'd seen it time and again. Children needed educating, but their parents, usually the father, deemed to need them more.

Mrs Baker continued. "Thomas Walker is another of the older boys. He's a strong lad, and is a hard worker, according to his mother."

How could she teach children who weren't allowed to attend? She was fighting a lost cause, and she hadn't even started work yet.

She finished up her breakfast without another word, then prepared to leave. Why did she even bother? It was the same story in every town she'd attempted to teach at. Numbers constantly dwindled, and supplies were often not available.

Victoria thought about all the other occupations she could have taken up, and wondered why this one appealed so much.

"Have a lovely day, Victoria," Mrs Baker said as she opened the front door. "Don't be too disheartened. I'm sure you'll do your best." She nodded, forced a smile, and headed toward the makeshift school.

Victoria turned the corner and was confronted by a small crowd of children and adults alike. She took a deep breath and let it out slowly.

She had arrived early to prepare her first lesson in peace, but it wasn't to be. "Good morning," she said to the crowd. "I am Miss Victoria Hudson. I will be teaching your children."

"This is Mary," one mother said, pushing her daughter forward. "She can count but she can't read or write."

Another child was shoved toward her. "Johnny can read some and write a little. I've done the best I can with the time I have available."

"Of course," Victoria said, guiding the teenage boy inside. What else could she say?

The words all became one massive gaggle as everyone suddenly spoke at once. She stood on the steps to the makeshift school and addressed all the parents at once. "I promise to look after your children, and teach them well."

"We ain't had a teacher here before," one woman said. "I hope you're gonna stay long enough to learn 'em good."

Victoria winced inside. She hated to think what she would be dealing with, but it was good to be here. Grand Falls seemed like a wonderful place to live and to bring up a family. It was a terrible shame the children had not been granted an education before this.

But that would all change now. She would make sure of it.

"Thank you for bringing your children along. Please return this afternoon to collect them." She nodded, then turned and entered the school.

Taking a deep breath as she closed the door behind her, Victoria felt as though she'd been confronted by an angry mob. She knew the parents all meant well, but it was not how she thought her morning would progress.

She spun around and faced the children who had each found a seat.

"Good morning, children." She smiled as best she could given the circumstances of a few minutes ago

– she felt thoroughly rung out. "I am Miss Hudson, and I am your teacher."

"Good morning, Miss Hudson," they all chanted together.

Today was the beginning of a new day, and a new adventure. She would teach these children to read and write if it was the last thing she did.

The first day was always the hardest, she knew that from past experience. Having no knowledge of her new pupils had always proved challenging.

With the introduction out of the way she could relax.

"Please tell me your names, starting with you." She pointed to the teenage boy sitting at the back.

He stood. "Johnny Ambrewster, Miss."

She was glad to see he'd made it, despite Mrs Baker's prediction.

"Mary Higgins."

"Anna Meyer."

They continued until every child had given their name. They were a small group of only seven and ranged in ages. She wondered how much each child had previously learned. That would be a task in itself, and a challenge for her as their teacher.

"Thank you everyone. I will learn your names quickly, I promise."

She pulled out seven slates and handed them out with a piece of chalk and a rag for each child. "I would like you to write your name on the top, then solve a simple sum." The children looked up in expectation, but Victoria noticed not one of them had written their name.

"Please write your name before we begin." Except for two boys, the students all wriggled in their seats and glanced at each other. It was rather perplexing.

"Please Miss Hudson," Johnny said, his words uncertain. "This is our first day of school."

"Oh," she said rather deflated. "You've not been to school all year? That's disappointing."

"No, Miss." Roy O'Hara stood this time. "It's our first day of school ever." He looked down at his feet. "Most of us don't know how to write our names."

So what the mother had said was true. She had hoped the woman had been stretching the truth.

"Roy and me, we can write our names and read a little, but not the others," Johnny Ambrewster added.

This was going to be more challenging than she'd ever imagined. Not only were most of her students illiterate, but according to Mrs Baker, they likely wouldn't attend school on a regular basis.

She wanted to run, to take the train back from where she'd come, but that would be quitting. She might be a lot of things, but Victoria Hudson was no quitter.

Challenge accepted.

Chapter Three

Jesse stood back and stared at his handiwork. The store looked pretty good, if he did say so himself.

He'd done his very best to replicate the layout of Uncle Joshua's store. He figured it would make it far easier to find his supplies that way.

He certainly didn't want to keep customers waiting while he tried to recall where everything was. This way it would be seconds rather than minutes to locate necessary items.

The bell over the door jingled and he looked up. His first customer.

"Oh." It was Mrs Baker. He smiled – he wasn't unhappy to see her.

"I'm sorry to disappoint you," she said, mirth in her voice. "I did come to buy something if that counts."

He brightened up. "That most certainly counts," he said, and straightened his tie. He didn't want to appear sloppy.

She glanced around the room. "Very impressive, Mr Pendleberry. One would assume you are a trained apothecarist?"

She meant nothing by it, he was certain. Mrs Baker was one of those people who needed to know facts.

"Of course. I trained under my uncle – Joshua Pendleberry. I completed my four-year apprenticeship under him, trained for an additional five years, then successfully sat all my exams. I've been fully qualified for many years now." He pointed to a certificate hanging on the wall. "That's my certificate of qualification if you would like to check."

He watched as she nodded her approval. "Wonderful!" she said, rubbing her hands together. "You wouldn't happen to have an ointment I could use for burns? I'm forever burning myself at the diner."

He reached into a glass cabinet and pulled out two jars. "This is the one I recommend for burns, Mrs Baker. I have a large or small size, as you can see."

"I'll take the larger size, thank you."

He pulled the lid off the ceramic jar and offered it to his customer. She leaned closer and breathed in the fragrance. "It doesn't smell too ghastly," she said.

He grinned. "I mostly make my own potions. I added lavender oil to this one to mask the dreadful smell."

His very first customer handed over payment, and he opened the door for her. "Thank you, Mrs Baker. I hope to see you again soon."

"Oh you will, young man. I can assure you of that."

She waved as she strolled down the boardwalk toward the diner. He closed the door and began to whistle. Perhaps this move was worthwhile after all.

Jesse hadn't found time to visit the Mercantile, so planned to eat at the diner. Not that he felt like cooking – he was still quite exhausted from his trip here as well as preparing the store for its opening.

The few customers he'd had that day all recommended it mostly highly.

His mouth watered just thinking about it. Alas, he needed to get food out of his mind. His working day was not yet over. He reached for his pestle and mortar, left to him in Uncle Joshua's will. He was also left his uncle's formularies, which contained all of his recipes, and a substantial amount of cash. It was as though his uncle knew Samson wouldn't allow him to take over the family business.

The fact left his cousin bristling, but there was nothing he could do about it. Jesse smiled at the thought. His smile soon left him at the thought of his dear uncle and his shocking death.

The bell over the door tinkled. "Good afternoon," he said as he glanced up. "I am Doctor Jesse Pendleberry. How may I help you?"

The older woman looked him up and down, and glanced around the store. "You look to be well stocked, young man." She stepped forward. "I am Mrs Esther Davis. You can call me Mrs Davis."

He grinned.

"Edna, that is, Mrs. Baker recommended you and your store, so I decided to come and take a look."

He stood a few steps closer, but not so many to overwhelm the woman. "Does something ail you, Mrs Davis?"

"My husband has terrible pain in his back." She pointed to the area. "Doc Spencer suggested Laudanum, but my Ralph rejected it. He still wants to function, after all."

"How bad is the injury, Mrs Davis? Do you think perhaps Mr Davis might come and see me?"

"Oh goodness no. He is in far too much pain to travel." Her face stiffened. The woman was obviously upset at the situation her husband found himself in. "He's done heavy lifting most his life. Well, at least he did – I convinced him to employ someone this last summer."

She fiddled with her gloves. "We don't need the money, but we do need the business to continue running smoothly. We can't have it going to ruin after all these years."

He thought for a moment. "I could give you a liniment, Mrs Davis, but I think mustard plasters would work far better."

Her face brightened. "Oh, that would be marvelous."

He pulled out a drawer, and reached for his pestle and mortar. "It will take about half an hour, maybe a little longer. Do you have somewhere you can wait?"

This was the sort of thing he enjoyed. To be able to help people with their individual ailments gave him such satisfaction.

"I'll wait at the diner, and come back later." She turned to leave. "I really do appreciate your help, Doctor Pendleberry."

He opened the door, and she was gone.

Jesse had a good feeling about this town. The people were nice, lovely in fact, and business was already brisk.

The long journey was already proving to be worthwhile. And then there was Miss Victoria Hudson…

Deep in thought, Victoria strolled along the boardwalk.

Her first day at school had been more than a little distressing. How could parents allow their children to remain illiterate? To not even teach them to spell their own names was shameful.

Then she remembered what Mrs Baker had told her – children were expected to help their parents work the land. With the majority of parents illiterate themselves, how could they teach their children?

Victoria groaned.

She would have to start from scratch – teach each child the alphabet, then once they'd mastered that, how to spell their name.

Tears forced their way through. Not for herself and the additional work involved, but for those dear children who had been forced to work for their parents and live the life of adults.

She dearly wished she had been warned of the situation – she could have brought appropriate text books with her.

She praised The Lord she'd had the forethought to bring a set of the Elementary Spelling Book with her. She had enough copies for every child to have their own, and then some.

Perhaps a large chalkboard attached to the wall would help. Her hope was the preacher wouldn't object. These dear children needed visuals. Something to remind them of the daily teachings.

Victoria startled as she heard her name being called. "Miss Hudson. Oh, Miss Hudson." She glanced around to find the source.

Across the street Mr Pendleberry stood outside his store. "I trust you enjoyed your first day, Miss Hudson?"

There was so much she could tell him, but she chose not to engage with the man. "Yes, thank you," she said, a false smile on her face, then continued to her destination.

"I'm pleased to hear it," he called, as she disappeared down the street and toward the diner. Mrs Baker had informed Victoria she would be eating at the diner each night. Since her hostess would be there most nights, it made sense.

She did of course object, saying she could cook for herself, but the older lady would have none of it. Besides, what else was she to do with her 'spare' time? She had already spent over an hour at the makeshift school preparing lessons for the following day.

Her biggest hope was the children all turned up again.

Approaching the diner, she watched as a number of customers entered the building. Until now, she hadn't realized how popular the diner was. Her biggest fear now, was taking away space for a paying customer.

Oh! Perhaps she should offer to pay, but Victoria already knew Mrs Baker would be offended if she did.

She moved toward the diner door and slowly opened it. Mrs Baker was there to greet her. "Ah, Victoria! I was beginning to worry." She glanced about as she spoke. "Did you have a good day?"

"It was rather eventful," she said truthfully.

Mrs Baker looked taken aback. "In a good way, I hope." She waited expectantly for an answer.

Victoria shrugged her shoulders. "Sort of."

"Oh dear. Let's get you seated." She led Victoria to a seat at the back by a window. It was the only small table still available.

"Is it always this busy?"

"Not always." She handed over a menu, and left Victoria to herself. It was a bit of an eyeopener, as she wasn't aware the town was this large. Or perhaps some of these customers were from out of town. Either way, there were surely far more children in the area than the seven who had attended school that day.

It was more than a little disappointing, but knowing what she knew now, perhaps it was the best outcome at this time.

She read through the menu without really absorbing it, and Mrs Baker returned before she'd made a decision. "Have you decided yet?" she asked gently.

Victoria sunk down in her chair. "I think my brain is taking a vacation. What do you suggest?"

The older lady's eyebrows rose. "Our hearty soup with bread is always popular, so is the steak."

"I'll have the hearty soup, thank you." It did sound delicious.

She glanced up as the door to the diner opened. Mrs Baker left her to see to her new customer. She craned her neck to see if it was anyone she knew. Not that she knew many people.

Victoria groaned as she saw Mrs Baker heading her way. She slunk back down in her chair as she recognized Mr Pendleberry trailing behind her.

"You don't mind, do you, my dear? We are rather busy tonight."

She plastered a smile on her face. "Of course not. Hello again Mr Pendleberry."

"Good evening to you, Miss Hudson," he said cordially. She was certain he was forcing his greeting as much as she had done.

He was handed a menu and quickly made a decision. "Steak, if you don't mind, Mrs Baker."

She grinned. "Men do like their steak." She chuckled as she walked toward the kitchen. It was only a short time later when a waitress returned with a plate of bread and some butter.

"How was your opening day, Mr Pendleberry?"

"Very good," he said, grinning. "Far better than I'd expected, to be honest, Miss Hudson." He offered her the bread first, then took a piece for himself. He leaned in closer. "I've been told by several customers the food here is wonderful."

"I've experienced Mrs Baker's food at home. It is rather special," she whispered.

He grinned. "Tell me, Miss Hudson, how was *your* first day?"

She knew it shouldn't, but it made Victoria feel rather deflated, and she sighed.

"Oh dear," he said before she even had a chance to respond. "Was it that bad?"

"Seven children turned up, so that was a blessing," she said quietly. "But they informed me they've never attended school before. Only two of them can write their name, Mr Pendleberry!"

He looked astounded. "Seriously?"

"It was devastating. They also don't know the alphabet." She shook her head sadly. "It is heartbreaking," she told him.

The waitress arrived with their food before he had a chance to respond, but Victoria knew from his expression he was equally as concerned as she was.

"The food looks delicious," he said, then leaned it. "It smells delicious too."

"It certainly does." She lifted her cutlery, and Mr Pendleberry followed suit.

"Oh, wait," he said quickly. "Shall we give thanks for our food before we start?"

She nodded her acceptance, and he reached over and gently held her hands. Warmth shot through her, and Victoria admonished herself for her body's unwanted reaction.

"We give thanks for this food, Dear Lord, and for our present company. We would also like to pray for the children, that you guide Miss Hudson in her endeavors to teach them, and mold them into productive adults. Amen."

When he let go of her hand, a chill crept through her. As much as she didn't want to admit it, just a touch from Mr Pendleberry had sent a shiver scurrying through her.

She glanced across at him. "That was very kind of you," she said, then once again picked up her cutlery, this time taking a mouthful of the soup. "It's wonderful," she said, putting her spoon down in the bowl.

He waved his hand about as he chewed. "This is literally melting in my mouth. I can see I will go broke eating here most nights."

They both laughed. It was then Victoria realized Mr Pendleberry wasn't the brute she'd first thought he was.

After dessert, they enjoyed a cup of coffee together, and he offered to take a stroll with his eating companion. Perhaps they could see a little more of the town and he could then accompany her home?

Mrs Baker told them she would finish up in about an hour, which gave them time to carry out their plans, and perhaps arrive home around the same time as their hostess.

As they left, he went to pay for both their meals, but Mrs Baker would have none of it. "You have been most generous with your time and your money in getting Miss Hudson's luggage delivered." He scowled. "Consider it a gift just this once."

"I reluctantly accept," he said. "But only this one time, and only because you insist."

She grinned at him.

"Thank you, Mrs Baker. We are off for our stroll now. Anything we should avoid?"

"Not really. Grand Falls is generally very safe." He nodded and they began to walk away. "Oh, Mr Pendleberry!"

He turned back. "I did mean to say that ointment you sold me today is excellent. I've already used it on a burn and it was the best I've ever used. Thank you."

He beamed. "I am very pleased to hear it," he said, then crooked his arm for Victoria to escort him through the door.

"Sounds like your concoctions are popular already," she told him, then winced the moment the words were out. "I'm sorry. I didn't mean it to sound so awful."

He chuckled. "Don't apologize. I've heard far worse." He patted her hand and continued along the boardwalk.

"Oh?"

"Apparently I'm a witch doctor."

Victoria stared at him open-mouthed. "You're kidding, right?" He shook his head and she stared in disbelief. "People can be cruel. And stupid. That doesn't even make sense."

He looked to the ground. "No, it doesn't. I studied for five years to get my degree. Five whole years. Before that, I studied under my uncle as his apprentice." He kicked at the ground with his shoe. "I can do nearly everything a regular doctor can do. Heck, I have a certificate that says I am a doctor!"

Her heart ached for him. They were alike in so many ways. "I have similar problems, but not like yours," she said. Then stopped. What she encountered was nowhere near as bad as being called a witch doctor.

It was as though he read her mind. "Please tell me."

She shook her head. "I spoke out of turn. Your situation is far worse."

He led her to a wooden bench and they sat down. "Please?"

He seemed sincere in every way. Had she misjudged the man? She truly hoped she had, because she'd had him pegged to be far worse than what he now seemed. Victoria sighed. "Women teachers cannot get permanent appointments. We also can't get long-term contracts – preference is always given to men."

"Well, that's not fair!" He said aggressively and frowned.

"If we marry, we have to resign."

"Who makes these stupid rules?" He was far from happy, and let it be known. "How long are you here for? I never did ask."

Victoria stared at him. He hadn't asked, but neither had she offered. "I have a one-year contract, but if a male teacher wants my job, I have to leave quietly."

Shock was apparent in his expression. "Truly?"

This was not a conversation she'd expected to have with Mr Pendleberry. Not tonight and not ever. "It's true – I wouldn't lie about something like that."

His words were soft, gentle. "You wouldn't lie about anything, I'm absolutely certain."

He patted her hand again, then began to stand, taking her with him. "Shall we take another stroll?"

She nodded her agreement, and they set off again. Without her consent, Victoria was beginning to like Mr. Jesse Pendleberry. When she first met him on the train, she considered him a scoundrel of sorts. He was proving to be far different.

Victoria was certain she needed to protect her heart or risk losing it to the man standing beside her.

Chapter Four

Jesse knew from the moment he laid eyes on her that Miss Victoria Hudson was special.

She was often funny, but could also be very serious. He listened very carefully as she explained her predicament, just as she'd listened to him.

He'd liked her from the moment he'd seen her. It had come to a head when she began making faces as she sat opposite him in the carriage.

He had to admit, he'd never met anyone like her before.

Not that he'd met many women socially. Of course he'd come across hundreds as he worked in his uncle's apothecary – spanning several years.

Uncle Joshua had encouraged him to date, but his studies were far more important. He knew the work he did was important, and put all his efforts into his work and his training.

He didn't expect anything less of himself. Nor did his uncle.

Much to cousin Samson's disgust, his uncle had paid upfront for Jesse's tuition. It wasn't cheap by any means, but he was determined to pay every cent back, and had done so well before his uncle's untimely death.

If nothing else, he was a man of honor. Far too much for his own good. He had almost married Melanie Wingate, even after she'd blatantly lied to him – and everyone else. They were happily engaged, at least he thought they were until he discovered she was also stepping out with Horace Bligh.

The day she accused him of causing her pregnancy was the day he found out she'd been cheating on him. Since he knew she was lying, but couldn't prove it, he felt compelled to marry her, despite it leaving a bitter taste in his mouth.

For once in his life, Horace had owned up and walked her down the aisle. Last he heard they were still together. Their baby would have to be at least two now. It seemed to have been the making of Horace, so that had to be a good thing.

Jesse knew he'd had a lucky escape. There was no way he could trust Melanie after such an atrocious lie.

He shook himself. He didn't want to think of such dreadful things, especially after a most pleasant evening with Miss Hudson.

As they approached the house, it was obvious Mrs Baker was now home. Light from the lanterns showed in the window, and he could see her silhouette through the drapes as she wandered about.

It was time to say goodnight to his dining companion, but he really didn't want to. He'd enjoyed her company far too much, and wondered if she had enjoyed spending her evening with him.

"Thank you for a lovely evening, Mr. er, Dr. Pendleberry," she said quietly as they reached the front door.

He stared at her momentarily. Her eyes were every bit as pretty in the moonlight, if not more, than during the daylight hours.

As she stood in the doorway, he felt compelled to lean in and kiss her full lips, but knew there was every possibility he would have his face slapped should he try.

A smile curled his lips.

"What's so funny?" Her words came out of the darkness.

He continued to stare, his heart thudding in his chest and his gut twisted in knots. "I'm thinking about kissing you," he said softly, then lifted his hand and caressed her cheek.

"I, I'm not sure if I should let you," she said quietly, her voice slightly teasing.

"In that case…" He leaned forward to take his prize when suddenly the front door opened.

Victoria pulled the covers up under her chin. Not that she was cold, instead it was comforting.

She was so close to being kissed by a man. It was the first time any man had ever felt compelled to kiss her. She would cherish that moment forever.

She didn't blame Mrs Baker for interrupting them. She wasn't to know, and had no idea what was happening on the other side of the door.

She sighed. Perhaps it was for the better. If she found herself romantically involved, she could lose her posting. Then what would she do?

Closing her eyes, she pictured Dr Pendleberry leaning in toward her, his eyes sparkling in the moonlight. He was certainly a good looking man. Ruggedly handsome was a term she'd heard used in the past, and that suited him perfectly.

She rolled over and tried to sleep, but sleep was elusive. Her heart beat wildly just thinking about what could have been.

Would he try to kiss her again? The thought of his arms wrapped around her was exhilarating. She didn't dare think what his lips on hers would feel like.

Her mind was racing with the possibilities. If she wasn't tucked up in bed, Victoria was certain she would swoon right about now.

With a sliver of moonlight shining through the gap in the curtains, she rolled over and tried once more to sleep. The last thing she recalled before sleep claimed her was thinking of Dr Jesse Pendleberry and what the future might hold for two of them.

Jesse stood outside the entrance to his store and waited.

Miss Hudson would eventually have to walk past to get to the makeshift school. He only wanted to catch a glimpse of her, say hello, and then return to his store.

He felt like a heartsick teenager. What was it about her that turned his brain to mush? When she literally fell into his arms on the train, he knew.

Knew that she was the one. Except she'd taken a very distinct dislike to him. Jesse knew he was a bit of a prankster, and it did put some people off, but he liked to say things the way they were.

It had gotten him into more than a bit of trouble over the years.

Oh, he was never rude to people, that just wasn't him. But telling Miss Hudson she'd made a gruesome face probably wasn't the smartest thing he'd ever done.

She had quite obviously taken offense at his words, and he wasn't sure she'd forgiven him, even now.

He glanced up – there she was. His whole body flooded with warmth.

She stood tall and strolled along the boardwalk and headed right for him. Well, not for him exactly. She was on the other side of the street, and it was plain for all to see she was making her way to the church hall where classes were being held.

She looked so pretty this morning. The gown she wore was made of a deep red material, velvet perhaps, and had long sleeves that ruffled at the wrist. Similar ruffles adorned the hem of the garment. The collar was high and there were small white buttons from the neckline to the waist, and what a tiny waist it was. Her head was adorned with a black bonnet and silk flowers of red that matched her outfit.

He glanced up to see her staring at him. He waved, and was rewarded with a smile.

Against his better judgement he continued to stare until she turned the corner toward the church. When she was finally out of sight, his heart rate began to calm down.

"You're not interested in our Miss Hudson, are you?"

The question came out of the blue, and so did the person saying it. "Why, of course not, Mrs Baker." He near stuttered, reaffirming his assessment he was acting like a lovestruck teenager.

"Hmph!" She glared at him for a few seconds, then her face softened. "She could do worse, but do you know how difficult it is to get a school teacher to these parts?"

He shook his head.

"Especially one as good as Miss Hudson." She glared at him again, then leaned in and whispered. "Please leave her alone."

Jesse swallowed. Had he just been warned off? He thought perhaps he had. "I, uh…"

"Enough of that. Inside with you, I need your help."

Mrs Baker was the last person he expected to want perfume, but she did indeed. "Why not?" she'd said, and he totally agreed.

By the time she left Mrs Baker had a large brown paper bag full of perfume, skin lotion, and herbal teas. The latter for the diner, she'd told him. In the space of a few days, she'd become his best customer, so he threw in some lip salve for good measure.

He knew that wouldn't change her mind. She would likely hound him if he pursued the fascinating Miss Victoria Hudson.

It was day four of school, and Victoria gave each child a copy of the Elementary Spelling Book, writing their name on the front inside page before handing it over.

"Now children, I want you to copy your name onto the slate. Write it as many times as you can fit."

Repetition was going to be the key here. The more times they wrote their name, the easier it would become.

She strolled around the room checking out each child's handiwork. The more she checked, the more disheartened she became.

This simply wasn't working.

"Alright children, you can clean your slates and we will try something else." She waited until everyone had wiped their slate clean. "We're going to practice the alphabet. Turn the pages of your book until you come to this page."

She held up her copy of the book she'd handed out earlier. "I want you to copy the letters in the left-hand column. They are the *lowercase* letters."

Once again, she wandered around the room. This was one of the smallest classes she'd taught, but because few of them knew how to write, it was proving difficult.

Perhaps even beyond her capabilities.

Victoria shook herself. She couldn't think like that – these children needed her help.

She flinched as she heard the sound of something smashing. "Maude O'Gorman, you pick up that broken slate. Don't you ever treat your school equipment like that again!" She admonished herself for using such a tone with a child, but knew she was at the end of her tether.

"Yes, Miss. Sorry, Miss."

Victoria turned her back to fetch another slate, and was startled by screaming. Suddenly it was like a gaggle of geese – everyone was talking at once.

The girls were crying, the boys were shouting. Young Maude was bleeding everywhere.

"Oh, Lordy be," she said under her breath. "Johnny, can you fetch Mr Pendleberry please? Tell him it's urgent, and we need bandages."

"Mr Pendleberry?"

"At the new Apothecary. Do you know where that is?"

"Yes, Miss." And with that he was gone.

This was all her fault. She'd pushed the children far too much, and they weren't ready. Victoria looked around for something to use to stem the bleeding. There was nothing.

She lifted her gown and ripped one of her skirts. There was no other choice, she had to try and stop the flow of blood, or the little girl could die.

She quickly wrapped the makeshift bandage around the child's hand. No matter what she did, blood seeped all the way through.

"Miss, I feel dizzy," Maude said quietly.

She glanced about. "Walter, you and Roy push some of those chairs together for a makeshift bed. We need to lay her down."

The boys did exactly as they were told.

She spun around as the door opened. "Oh, Mr Pendleberry, thank goodness you're here."

"It's Dr Pendleberry," Johnny told her gently.

"Of course. I apologize…"

He waved her words aside. "No matter." He glanced at the pool of blood on the floor, and then to Victoria. He rushed to his patient, and began to check her injury. "Mr. Ambrewster," he said firmly. "Please remove one of the smaller bandages from my bag, and a packet of gauze dressing, and take them out of the packaging. Do you know what that is?" he asked as he removed the makeshift bandage.

"Yes, Sir." He began to unwrap them.

"This is going to hurt, little one, but I have to do it." He gently opened her hand to better see the cut, then winced. The bleeding began again. "I will need that gauze dressing first, if you don't mind."

"Yes, Sir."

Everyone stood around watching his every movement. "We need a little space, children." They all took a few steps back. "What is your name, Sweetheart?"

She sniffled. "Maude."

"Miss Maude, I'm going to put pour some liquid on your cut, and then this dressing." She nodded.

"Mr Ambrewster, please pass the witch hazel water. It's not the best thing for cuts, but it's the best I have at such short notice."

"Yes, Sir. Is this it?"

"It most certainly is. Thank you." He opened the bottle and poured the liquid over the cut.

Maude screamed the moment the liquid hit her skin, and Dr. Pendleberry tried to soothe her. "It's alright, Miss Maude," he said gently. "I will only sting for a tiny moment. See?" He said as she stopped screaming.

Victoria watched, captivated by his ministrations.

"I'm adding the dressing now, Miss Maude, and then the bandage." He watched her until she nodded her agreement.

Blood seeped through the dressing. "Mr Ambrewster, another gauze dressing if you will." He held Maude's hand up in the air and Victoria watched as the blood flow slowed. "There should be some paper bags in there for the rubbish." He nodded toward the bag.

One thing Victoria had learned today – Jesse Pendleberry was good at his job. In fact, he was more than good, he was brilliant.

Tears ran down Maude's face, but she said not a word. "You will be alright, Miss Maude, I promise. Don't you concern yourself." He gently brushed her tears away with the back of his hand.

Warmth flooded Victoria at his gentle touch and the way he cared for this young child who was obviously distressed.

"I'm ready for the bandage now," he told Johnny, and Victoria breathed a sigh of relief. If he needed the bandage, it must mean the bleeding had stopped.

Once the bandage was in place, he tied Maude's hand up against her chest. "This will stop it bleeding again," he told her gently. "You can take it off before you go to bed. Understand?"

The little girl looked up at him with tears in her eyes. "Yes, Sir."

Now the emergency was over, he squatted down to her level and pulled the child close, rubbing her back, trying to comfort her.

"Thank you, Dr. Pendleberry. I don't know what we would have done without you."

He turned to her and smiled. "Anytime." Then he turned to Johnny. "Mr. Ambrewster," he said, and the boy stood to attention. "How old are you?"

"Thirteen, Sir. I'll be fourteen at the end of the year."

Dr Pendleberry looked thoughtful. "You were a great help just now. I could use someone like you to assist me in the store, and with deliveries and such. But there's a problem, I need someone who can read and write."

"I can read and write some, and Miss Hudson is teaching us." He grinned across at her.

Victoria watched the exchange between the pair. What a wonderful opportunity for the boy, and a huge incentive to learn.

Dr Pendleberry nodded. "You come and visit me after school today, and we'll have a chat." Johnny grinned broadly. "I need someone who can read labels, and read them well. One other thing, your parents have to agree."

"Yes, Sir!" Johnny said proudly.

What a wonderful thing Dr Pendleberry was doing for this boy. She couldn't be prouder – of them both.

Chapter Five

"You'll need to study hard, Johnny. What I'm offering you is not like working at the Mercantile."

Johnny nodded.

"It's an important job, people rely on accuracy for their medications."

The boy frowned. "What if I kill someone, Sir?"

He looked totally serious. Jesse hadn't killed anyone yet, and doubted he ever would.

"Follow me." He took the boy behind the counter. "See this huge tome? This was passed to me by my uncle. He taught me everything I know – along with the formal training, of course."

Johnny stared at the book in his hands.

"This book contains recipes for all the lotions and potions you see around this room."

Johnny's eyes opened wide in astonishment. "Can I see?"

"No, I can't do that. You're not qualified. What if you tried to make one of the potions and got the ingredients wrong?"

He nodded his agreement. "I'm sorry, Sir."

"Don't be sorry. Here's the plan. You study hard at school, and learn to read and write well. You can't do this job otherwise."

"I promise to work hard, Sir."

"In the meantime, if your parents agree, I'd like you here for an hour after school every day." Again the boy's eyes opened wide. "There will be some deliveries, but when there's time, you can sweep the floor and learn where everything goes – in preparation for when you become my apprentice."

Johnny's jaw dropped open. "Your apprentice? Thank you, Sir." His eyes filled with tears, but he did a good job of fighting them back.

It was funny how things turned out. If it hadn't been for the disaster at the school today, Jesse would likely have never met this young lad. He'd have never seen the potential in him, and wouldn't have seen how calm he was under pressure. Above all, he wouldn't have found a future apprentice.

"Johnny," Jesse said firmly. "You didn't ask what I will be paying you."

"You're going to pay me?" The boy looked surprised.

Jesse couldn't help but grin. "Since you'll only be here for one hour a day, it won't be much. How does three dollars a week sound?"

The boy flew at him and wrapped his arms tightly around him. "Thank you, Sir. You don't know what this means to me."

He glanced down at the young boy who held on as though his life depended on it. "Believe me, I do, Johnny. Someone did the same thing for me once."

"What you did today was remarkable."

Jesse brushed her words aside. "Anyone would have done the same."

"I'm sure they wouldn't have. Doc Spencer is too far out of town, and you are far more convenient to the school. Maude could have bled to death by the time the Doc arrived."

Mrs. Baker sidled up beside them. "The whole town is talking about how you saved Maude's life," she said, handing them each a menu.

Victoria watched as he blushed.

"It wasn't like that," he objected.

"It absolutely was like that," she said. "I was terrified. I was convinced she would bleed out before help arrived." She reached across and covered his hand, then squeezed it.

He glanced up at Mrs. Baker, then swiftly pulled his hand away. "It's what I've been trained to do," he said.

"Oh, and did you hear what he's doing for Johnny?" she asked Mrs. Baker.

The woman shook her head. "No, but do tell."

"Promised him an apprenticeship if he learns to read and write properly."

"How wonderful!"

"It truly is," Victoria said. "It's a wonderful incentive for the boy to learn. I am so proud of the both of them."

"It's not that big of a deal, Miss Hudson," he said quietly.

"It is in this town," Mrs.Baker said. "Do either of you know what you're having?" she said.

"I'll have the hearty soup again if you don't mind." Victoria said.

"Steak for me, thanks."

Mrs. Baker rolled her eyes and walked away.

"I really do appreciate everything you did today, Dr. Pendleberry. I was in a right panic before you arrived. And so were the children, especially the younger ones."

"Could we change the subject? I feel uncomfortable getting all this praise for simply doing my job."

She watched him carefully and he squirmed in his chair. He didn't want this kind of attention for simply doing his job. "Since you insist. Tell me what you require of Johnny. What level of competence does he need?"

He frowned. "He needs to be completely fluent in the English language, and needs to able to read effortlessly."

"That makes sense. I will work with him, and ensure he works hard toward his goal."

Their food arrived and they said a prayer of thanks for the food as they had the previous night. Tonight though, Jesse added a prayer for a quick recovery for young Maude.

It was nice not having to eat alone, and to spend time with Victoria was an added bonus.

He hoped they would once again go for a stroll after supper tonight.

"I enjoy your company," Jesse said. "And wonder if you would accompany me on a stroll earlier in the evening sometime."

Victoria glanced across at him. "You don't like strolling around a strange place at night?" She grinned at him.

"I will go with you anytime, and anywhere," he told her truthfully. "I just thought it would be nice to go in the daylight for a change. We would get to know the place better."

She nodded. "Perhaps one Sunday, after church?"

"That sounds wonderful," he told her. "Shall we make it a date? After church next Sunday?" Excitement rushed through him and it made him pause. Was he so deprived of things to do in this town that taking a stroll with a woman who was practically a stranger excited him more than anything else he'd ever done?

He already knew the answer. It was not the stroll that excited him, but spending time with the charming Miss Hudson.

Just the thought of it made his heart beat wildly. He took in a slow breath trying to calm himself.

"A *date*, Dr Pendleberry?" She quirked an eyebrow at him.

Mrs Baker's words came back to him full force. "Ah, perhaps not a date as such, but a chance to get to know the town better."

"That does sound wonderful, Dr Pendleberry."

He glanced down at her and sighed. "Do you think we can dispense with the Dr Pendleberry business? I find it rather tiresome. You may call me Jesse."

She smiled. "In that case, you may call me Victoria."

They soon finished their first course, then ordered dessert. Mrs. Baker bought out cherry cobbler, Jesse's favorite. It was even topped with clotted cream.

"That looks amazing," he said before tucking in. He glanced up to see Victoria grinning. "What? It's delicious."

She chuckled and he put his spoon down momentarily. "You look like you've been starved, and I'm certain that isn't true." She grinned, so at least he knew she was joking.

"It's been a long time since I've eaten. Today was rather eventful, in case you hadn't noticed, and I forgot to eat lunch."

She did not look amused. "You need to eat. We need you to be strong and healthy."

Disappointment flooded him. Was that all she cared about? Did she not worry for his wellbeing for any other reason?

He truly hoped he was wrong. Jesse had to admit to developing feelings for Victoria – far more than just being friends.

The days seemed to fly by, and Sunday arrived before she knew it.

Victoria was sitting at the kitchen table drinking her tea when there was a knock at the door.

"Who on earth could that be?" Mrs Baker asked as she rushed around getting ready to leave.

Having no idea either, Victoria shrugged her shoulders. "Would you like me to answer the door?"

"Oh, thank you! That would be wonderful. Now where did I put my gloves?"

Holding back a grin, she went to the front door. "Oh, it's you!" She stared into the face of Jesse, and was not unhappy about it.

"I didn't expect to see you either," he said, grinning from ear to ear. "I thought perhaps I could accompany you ladies to church this morning."

She looked back over her shoulder but couldn't see Mrs Baker. "Wait a moment, if you will." She began to walk away. "Oh, I do apologize – please come in."

His eyes were laughing but his smile was being held back she was certain. "I'll wait here."

She wandered off to find Mrs Baker. "I'm almost ready, my dear," she said when told Dr Pendleberry had arrived to escort them to church.

For some reason, Mrs Baker did not seem too pleased at the news. Victoria had no idea why that would be. She and Jesse were no more than friends.

It wasn't long and they were on their way. As they turned the corner, Victoria had a sense of coming home. Whether or not that was because the school was operating out of the church hall, she wasn't sure.

One thing she did know, she couldn't believe it had already been more than a week since she'd arrived.

"Good morning, Miss Hudson!" Before she knew what was happening, Victoria was surrounded by her students.

"Good morning, children," she said, and was filled with warmth. "How is your hand, Maude?"

Maude glanced across to Jesse. "It's still sore, but Dr Pendleberry is looking after it." She ran over to Jesse and wrapped her arms around his legs.

He reached down and rubbed her back. "We're checking it every day, and it is far better than it was," he told her.

The child's parents came up and thanked Jesse for everything he'd done. "You don't have to keep thanking me," he told them. "I'm always happy to help."

Just then *Room at the Cross* began to play, and everyone made their way inside. Mrs Baker, being the social person she was, chose a seat near the middle, but Victoria would have far preferred being right at the back.

What choice did she have? She was under the guidance of Mrs Baker, so she and Jesse both followed her.

The church was packed and therefore the seats were full. They were closely packed on the seats, pushed closely together. Jesse's thigh touched hers, and she wasn't unhappy about it. She stretched forward and reached for one of the bibles, dropping it as she did so.

Luckily, Jesse caught it, so it wasn't damaged. The heat from his hands brushing against hers sent warmth rushing through her body. Victoria was not happy about this situation, especially given they were in church.

"Thank you," she said quietly, and he grinned.

Victoria loved it when he smiled. It always sent shivers down her spine. If she was certain she wouldn't be leaving Grand Falls in a year or less, she might consider stepping out with Jesse, but given her circumstances, it was not possible.

The service was nice. Pastor Devon welcomed all the visitors, and hoped everyone would join them after church for morning tea.

Excitement went through Victoria. Perhaps some of the other parents would be there, and she'd be able to recruit them to bring their children along to school? As she glanced about, she noticed there weren't a lot of children. The majority of those that were there, already attended.

As they made their way outside, she shook the pastor's hand. "It's so good to see you here," he said. "While I think of it, we found a large chalkboard in the back shed."

"Oh my goodness, that is marvelous," she said excitedly. "I was going to see if one could be made."

Pastor Devon leaned in. "I'll see if I can get a few of these strong young men to carry it to the hall for you." He winked as he glanced across at Jesse.

"I don't mind at all, Pastor Devon," he said, and Victoria was certain he didn't.

Mrs Baker came out not long after them – she'd been chatting to some of the auxiliary ladies. "Shall we get a cup of coffee?" she asked, not waiting for an answer.

Jesse glanced at her, and they both grinned. They were beginning to get used to Mrs Baker's antics. At least Victoria knew she was, and it seemed Jesse was too.

The ladies both sat at the back of the hall, and Jesse brought them a hot drink. He returned soon after with one of his own, and a small plate of refreshments to share.

"Grand Falls is a friendly sort of place," Jesse said. "Not too big and not too small."

"It's expanding all the time," Mrs Baker said, then sighed. "I loved it when it was just a tiny dot on the map, but it's almost getting too big for me. Not that I should complain, business is better than ever."

"It always seems busy when I've been there," Jesse said.

Mrs Baker nodded. "You haven't been there Saturday nights. I have to take bookings."

Jesse shook his head and was about to answer when the Mercantile owner interrupted them to introduce himself. "Cecil Delbert from the Mercantile," he said, shaking Jesse's hand.

"Pleased to meet you. I'm am Dr Jesse Pendleberry, from the Apothecary, and this is Miss Victoria Hudson," Jesse told him. "The new schoolmarm."

They chatted for a while, Mr Delbert thanking Jesse for looking after young Maude the way he did. "It's nice to know you're available in an emergency," he said. "Doc Spencer lives too far out of town to help sometimes."

It was a sentiment she'd heard before.

It wasn't long and it was time to go home for lunch. Mrs Baker said they were having a roast dinner, which was already in the oven, and invited Jesse to join them.

Victoria wasn't sure if that was a good idea. She was becoming far too enamored with the new apothecarist.

Chapter Six

Victoria pulled her shawl up around her shoulders. "It's a might chilly out this afternoon," she told Jesse, and he agreed.

"Do you want to go back for your coat?"

She shook her head.

He still wore his Sunday best suit, not having been back home after church. It was very nice of Mrs Baker to have invited him to lunch, and he made sure to tell her.

She stared at him momentarily as if to send a message. That message being *don't get too close to our schoolmarm*. He was more than certain of it.

Her warning earlier in the week had forced him to keep his distance, but Jesse wasn't sure how long he could keep up the charade.

He had found himself more than once wanting to pull Victoria into an embrace. He wanted to hold her close, and he *really* wanted to kiss her. She had such a pull on him, and it was hard to ignore it.

It wasn't just her beauty, though that was hard to miss. And it wasn't just her personality, which was big and enticing. There was far more to it. He'd been watching – everyone who met her seemed captivated by her.

She was also smart, and he thought perhaps that attracted him more than anything. He was certain they could make beautiful babies together.

Jesse stopped in his tracks. Where on earth had that come from?

"Is everything alright, Jesse?" she asked, as he stood there like a fool with no idea where he was going. "Jesse?"

He adored the way his name rolled off her tongue.

"What?" He glanced across at her. "Oh, sorry. My mind went blank for a minute there." There was no way he could tell her what he'd been thinking. He would have his face slapped for sure this time.

The thought made him smile. She was a feisty little lady, this schoolmarm, and he didn't dislike it. He rather enjoyed her antics. At least most of the time he did.

The hardest thing was keeping his distance. He hated the thought of not seeing her at all, but if Mrs Baker had her way, that's exactly what would happen.

"I've been thinking about Johnny Ambrewster," she said out of the blue. "I decided to give him some responsibility, let him help the younger children with their reading."

"How will that help?" It seemed rather back-to-front to him.

They continued to stroll along the boardwalk, arms hooked. "I've been doing it already. I thought it would make him want to become more proficient to help the others, while helping himself."

"Sounds feasible."

"It's definitely feasible," she said. "And it's already working."

"I don't doubt you," he said, glancing across at her. "Shall we venture out toward the livery? We might see a little more of the area."

Victoria nodded. He was certain she was as eager as he was to see the scenery surrounding Grand Falls.

As they arrived at the livery an older teenage boy loitered out the front. "Want to hire a buggy, Sir? Take the Missus for a ride?"

He glanced at Victoria. "What do you say?"

"It would be far too expensive," she said, so he turned to the boy.

"How much?"

"Two dollars for you, Sir, provided you're back before five. Otherwise me pa will have me hide."

Jesse reached into his wallet. "Make it three dollars and you have a deal."

They boy grinned. "Yes, Sir. Thank you, Sir," he said, then turned to prepare the buggy.

It was far too late by the time Jesse realized this was not him keeping his distance from the enchanting schoolmarm.

The buggy didn't allow much space between them, and Victoria found herself in close proximity to her riding companion.

When he'd helped her up onto the buggy, her body had near sizzled. When he'd sat next to her, an absolute thrill ran through her.

She took a long, calming breath. She may only have another six months out here, perhaps even less if a male teacher took a liking to her posting in Grand Falls.

"It's really beautiful here."

Jesse's voice brought her out of her thoughts, and had her looking around. "Yes, it really is. From town, the mountains look beautiful, but from up here, they are even more so."

He pulled into a clearing, and brought the buggy to a standstill. "Would you like to take a stroll?"

His eyes almost begged him, and she couldn't say no. "Absolutely. There's no point coming all this way unless we check it out properly."

He climbed down and hitched the horses to a nearby bush, then came around to help her down. Victoria braced herself. After her experience when he helped her up, she was certain it would happen again.

She looked down into his face as his arms outstretched. He looked far more serious than she felt he should be.

It was Sunday after all – their day off to do what they pleased.

She began to stand, but lost her balance and toppled toward him. She couldn't help herself – Victoria squealed.

He grabbed her around the waist and halted her fall. "You're safe," he said. "I won't let you fall." His eyes pierced hers, and she couldn't stop staring.

He slowly lifted her down to the ground, but she was still shaky, and again lost her balance. The uneven ground beneath her feet didn't help. He pulled her into his arms, no doubt to help her get her balance again.

It was nice, and everything she'd ever imagined it would be. She glanced up at him, and his eyes sparkled. "Are you alright?" His voice was soft but husky.

She leaned her head against his chest and rested there, trying to force her heartrate to calm down. Without thinking, she snaked her arms up around his back and held him tight.

He tightened his grip on her in response. "We shouldn't be doing this," he whispered. Since they were the only people there, Victoria had no idea why he spoke so softly.

"It is nice, though," she told him, her voice just as quiet.

He sighed. "Mrs Baker will be most unhappy."

His words confused her. What did Mrs Baker have to do with anything? "Mrs Baker?" She glanced up at him again. He looked far too concerned for her liking.

"Dear Mrs Baker warned me off you. Said it is far too hard to get school teachers out this way." Now he was grinning, as though it was a huge joke.

She pulled back and slapped his chest. "So the two of you have been plotting behind my back? How dare you!"

Victoria backed off and watched him continue to grin. "It is not funny," she said, heading for the buggy. She was a twenty-four year old woman who could make her own choices. No one else had the right to do that on her behalf. Not even Mrs Baker.

"Victoria," he called after her, but she was not in the mood for explanations. All she wanted to do now was go back home.

She stood with her arms crossed over her chest and her back to him. "How long have the two of you been plotting this?" She still didn't want to look at him, she was beyond angry.

He reached out and touched her shoulder. "There was no plot. It was a directive I was given." When she didn't pull away, he moved closer. Close enough he was able to wrap his arms around her.

As angry as she was right now, she enjoyed the feel of his arms around her. His body heat was comforting too. "It's none of her business," Victoria said under her breath.

He turned her around in his arms and pulled her closer. She molded into him. "What are we going to do," she asked quietly.

She glanced up at him, and a smile formed on his lips. "I know exactly what I'm going to do," he said, then leaned down and kissed her.

The chalkboard made a huge difference to the classroom and to the students. It now felt like a real classroom.

Of course it would be better if there was a dedicated school, but Victoria had taught in far less. One town had placed her into the unused storeroom of a saloon for the schoolhouse, which was not exactly pleasant, but they'd made do. They had no choice.

She glanced up to survey her students. Johnny Ambrewster sat in the corner listening to Maude read. It was an early learner book, and one she was certain he could manage. She longed for more books for the children to learn from, but for now, had to make do with what she had.

Walter sat quietly, not writing as he was meant to do, and she went over to help him. "Do you need help?"

He nodded. "I am practicing my name, but it doesn't look right."

"Here, let me write it for you again." She wrote his name legibly, and he copied it. Not perfectly, but he was getting there. Warmth filled her.

"Try that word again, Maude." Johnny's voice drifted across to her ears. "Sound it out if you need to."

She listened and didn't interrupt.

"A-p-p-l-e. Apple."

"Perfect," he said and smiled at her. Maude grinned at him.

Getting Johnny to help in the classroom was working. It was improving his own reading and writing. Working for Jesse was the encouragement he needed, and he was doing great.

He'd even helped her set up a reading corner with a bunch of cushions, to make it more comfortable. The whole class had helped decorate the room to make it more like a schoolroom, and they were finally settling in. They'd even had a few new students join them.

Victoria returned to her desk, and continued to work on her current project. She was creating banners that would be attached around the room. The set she worked on now were alphabet banners.

Each had a letter and a hand-drawn picture of an item that corresponded to that letter. She hoped the pastor didn't mind her putting them around the room.

When she'd finished these, she would make some with additions on them – easy sums, like one plus one equals two, two plus two equals four, and so on.

She smiled. Victoria was determined to give these children the education they deserved.

She waited until Maude had finished reading her book then stood. "It's lunch-time children. Grab your lunch-pails and take a break."

It was such a lovely day, she decided to go outside as well. She sat on the church steps and ate her sandwich, while she enjoyed a mug of tea. The children had all been working hard these past days, but none so much as Johnny Ambrewster. The boy was determined to win that apprenticeship Jesse had promised him if he could meet the conditions.

He was so determined that Victoria was certain he would.

She enjoyed the sun streaming down on her face as the children played. Another ten minutes and it would be time to go back inside.

As she enjoyed the sun, she heard a commotion and looked up. Jesse Pendleberry made his way toward her. "Is everything alright," she asked as she stood to greet him.

"Everything is perfect," he said. "I missed you, so decided to visit in the lunch-break."

She grinned, but knew she shouldn't. He stood beside her and put an arm around her shoulder.

"Ooooh, Miss Hudson has a boyfriend!"

They began chanting, and Jesse stood there grinning at her. He obviously thought it funny. She did not. Despite all that, she longed for his kiss. Was it really only yesterday since he'd first kissed her?

It was hard to believe, but it really was only one day earlier. They stood there for what seemed an eternity, until it was time for school to resume. The children all ran past them into the classroom.

Jesse turned to her. "I have to get back to work, and so do you." He looked none too pleased, but they both had work to do. He leaned in and kissed her. Right there, and on the lips.

That alone could cause a scandal if any of the children saw them.

The ruckus that followed confirmed they had. Victoria was certain she would never live it down.

Chapter Seven

The kiss they'd shared would be the beginning of something wonderful, Victoria knew it would.

She wasn't exactly pleased her students had witnessed Jesse kissing her, but it was what it was.

As they strolled around town that evening, she felt something she'd never felt before. It was happiness like no other she'd experienced before. She'd seen it with her parents so would recognize it anywhere.

The mere fact of being together brought sunshine into the other person's life. That's how she felt right now, walking beside Jesse, her arm hooked through his.

"Are you alright? You're very quiet," he said gently.

She nodded. "I'm more than alright. My happiness is overwhelming."

He stepped in front of her and pulled her into his embrace. "Jesse! Someone might see us," she said, but still rested her head on his chest. She felt safe in his arms, and never wanted to leave his embrace, but knew she had to.

It was not right to be standing here like this in the middle of town. The last thing she wanted was to set tongues wagging in Grand Falls. She was after all the schoolmarm. Under the conditions of her contract she had an image to uphold.

She wasn't even supposed to step out, not ever. It saddened her that she felt guilty every time she spent time with Jesse, because their relationship was beautiful, and innocent, and they shouldn't be made to feel this way.

At least this time of night was quiet. It was rare to come across other people, so they were relatively safe. Sneaking around like this made Victoria feel tainted, like she'd done something terribly wrong and had to hide it from the world.

It was horrid she was made to feel this way.

His hand gently caressed her cheek and she glanced up at him. "I have feelings for you, Victoria," he said quietly, his words caressing her as much as his fingers had touched her cheek just moments ago. "You are beautiful inside and out, and I want to spend the rest of my life with you."

She pulled out of his arms. "That's out of the question and we both know it." She stared at him. "You knew it even before you kissed me. There is nothing I can do about it."

He pulled her close to him again and hugged her tight. "I know, but it doesn't mean I'm happy about it," he said, then leaned in and kissed her like there was no tomorrow.

"Are you going to marry Miss Hudson?"

It was close to five weeks since the students witnessed their kiss. Since then he'd accompanied Victoria to dinner each night, and they'd strolled together each evening ever since. He'd even accompanied her to church and taken buggy rides after church each week.

He'd held her close and kissed her whenever the opportunity arose.

Still, he hadn't expected the words that seemed to come out of the blue. "Excuse me? Did you really ask that question, Mr Ambrewster?" Jesse near glared at the boy.

Johnny glanced up from his current project – stacking glass bottles the way Jesse preferred. He'd had a new shipment and no time to store them. It was something the boy needed to learn, so it was a good opportunity for them both.

He watched amused as heat crept up his protégé's neck and face. "Sorry, Sir." He ducked his head and went back to the task at hand.

"Are you enjoying your work, Mr Ambrewster?" Jesse continued to stir the potion in the pestle.

The boy stood. "Yes, Sir, I am. And I appreciate the opportunity."

"Then perhaps keep your mind on the job and not my love life. Understand?"

Johnny nodded. "Yes, Sir..." he said, but it was apparent he had more to say.

Jesse stopped what he was doing and addressed the boy again. "Out with it. This is your one and only opportunity to have your say, then it's back to work."

"Miss Hudson is a great teacher. None of us students want to lose her. If you marry her, she has to leave."

These were not the words of a thirteen year old. At least Jesse didn't think they were, so the boy's parents had been talking.

"Did you tell your parents I'd kissed Miss Hudson?"

Johnny's eyes opened wide. "No, Sir! I did not. There's talk around town 'bout you two steppin' out."

Great. Just what they needed – to be the butt of town gossip. Jesse sighed. "I like Miss Hudson, but as you know, she has to leave her job if she marries, so it can't happen."

Johnny didn't look happy. "But she likes you."

"I like her too, but I won't jeopardize her job, and I won't leave the students without a teacher. Now get back to work, Mr Ambrewster."

"Yes, Sir!" He squatted down again and got back to sorting the bottles.

"Now where was I?" Jesse said under his breath, and resumed work on his latest order.

The diner was reasonably quiet, and they sat waiting for their coffee.

Jesse leaned in and spoke quietly. "There's gossip going around about us," he said, then leaned back and waited for an answer.

"Gossip?" Victoria's heart thudded. Whatever could it be?

"Johnny asked if we're getting married," he said as he leaned in again.

Her eyes opened in astonishment. It was the last thing she expected Jesse to tell her. "Oh my. That is not good. I can talk to him tomorrow at school."

He shook his head. "Don't say anything. We've already had a talk. I don't think he'll breach the subject again. Apparently the word is we're stepping out together. It came from his parents."

It was even worse than she thought. "I'm going to lose my job," she said, terrified of exactly that happening. "I can't afford for that to occur. I'll never get another placement. Not ever." Tears were forming at the back of her eyes, but she wouldn't let them fall.

Jesse reached across and covered her hand with his. The moment skin met skin, warmth filled her. "What am I going to do?" She was now filled with despair. "Would it help if we stopped seeing each other?"

He shook his head. "I really don't want to do that. I really like you."

"I really like you too," she near whispered. "It is so unfair. If our roles were reversed, you could see whomever you wanted, even get married and it wouldn't matter."

"It is exceedingly unfair, I agree."

"I guess it's too late to pretend I'm a male teacher?"

The tiniest bit of a smile touched his lips, and had the circumstances been different, she knew he'd be grinning right now. It simply wasn't fair. They liked each other – a lot – and because of antiquated rules, she couldn't so much as socialize with a man who took an interest in her.

"If it would help, I'd suggest we get married right now." He looked serious, and if she didn't know better, she'd think he was serious.

"How would that help?"

He frowned. "At least it would stop the gossip, and people would leave us alone."

"But I'd still be out of a job." She brushed a stray tear from her eye.

He squeezed her hand. "It wouldn't bother me to support you. In fact, I'd be happy to do so."

Her heart rate kicked up, and Victoria didn't know what to say to that. "That all sounds very nice," she said gently. "Unfortunately it won't help my students."

He leaned in again. "What do you say? Why don't we get married? I could go see the preacher tomorrow and make the arrangements."

"Darn it, Jesse! You're not listening to me. That isn't going to help. My students need a teacher. From what I've been told, it's taken years for the town to secure a teacher. Me. And now that is in jeopardy." She sighed. "If I marry you, the children are right back where they started – including Johnny."

"I have big plans for that boy."

She sympathized with him. Johnny was a smart boy and could go a long way with the right help. "There is no other option. We have to stop seeing each other."

It had been two weeks since their last conversation, and the last time they'd spent time together.

Victoria was miserable. She pined for Jesse almost every waking moment, and barely slept at night. She had black shadows under her eyes, and concentration was difficult.

She'd never met anyone like him, and was certain she never would again.

Why on earth had she suggested they stop seeing each other?

For one, to ensure she retained her teaching position. The children of Grand Falls needed an education.

They'd gone for years without having formal education, and that just wasn't right. Johnny Ambrewster was a prime example. Thirteen years old and he had the most basic of reading and writing skills.

He was one of the lucky ones. His mother had taken the time to teach him in her spare time. She was a gem amongst a pile of rubble. Most of the parents around here had the most basic writing skills, if they could write at all, and were therefore unable to help their children.

Johnny was also good at arithmetic because he needed that skill on the farm, and had learned over the years.

She could see why Jesse had chosen him – apart from his other skills, the boy was calm under difficult circumstances. He'd proven that the day of Maude's accident.

She closed her eyes and rested her head on the pillow, but sleep was elusive, as it had been since that last evening they spent together. She pulled the covers up under her chin, then rolled to her side.

It made no difference. The sun was already rising in the sky, and so far she'd had not one wink of sleep. How did she expect to teach her students without being completely rested?

She might as well give in, and get up.

Victoria stoked the fire and got it burning nicely. The kettle was now close to the boil so she'd be able to make a cup of tea. She was looking forward to it.

While she waited, she put together a batch of biscuits, and slid them in the oven. It might still be

Spring, but it was certainly chilly at this hour of the day.

She'd enjoyed her cooking lessons with Mrs Baker, and was now proficient at several recipes. It would be a nice surprise for the lady whom she'd become quite close to over her time here so far.

At least she hoped it would be.

Checking the oven, the biscuits were done. They had a nice brown color to them, and their aroma was rather enticing.

She pulled the tray from the oven and placed them on the counter to cool.

With the sun now up over the horizon, she threw back the drapes to let in the daylight. It beat the soft glow of lanterns any day.

"Oh!" Victoria gasped as she glanced out the window. Standing across the road and staring toward her was Jesse. He looked as deflated as she felt.

Had it been anyone else standing there, it would have been creepy, but she knew exactly how Jesse was feeling.

She opened the front door and invited him in, her heart beating wildly in her chest. Was this even the right thing to do?

"I, I've just taken biscuits out of the oven, and the kettle is about to boil."

He took a step toward her and looked as though he was about to hug her, but stopped himself. She knew she shouldn't be, but Victoria was beyond disappointed. She had longed for his touch for so long, and now he was this close, he was still keeping his distance.

She motioned for him to enter the kitchen and sit. If nothing else, she would always be a good hostess.

She put butter on the table, and set plates and cutlery for three. Mrs Baker should be up soon.

Pulling mugs from the cupboard she turned to him. "Coffee or tea?"

He grinned. "Have you forgotten already? I only drink coffee."

She nodded. Of course she knew. It would be unlikely he'd change his drinking habits in such a short period of time. At least in reality it was short. To her mind, it felt like months.

She poured the coffee and sat it in front of him, pushing the sugar bowl closer, then placed a plate of biscuits in the center of the table.

Victoria sat in the chair nearest him. She wasn't sure why she did that – she'd managed to keep her distance all this time, but now he was here, she had to get as close as possible. It was the craziest thing she'd done in a long time. Except perhaps distancing herself from him.

"I supposed you're wondering why I was standing outside," he said, picking up a biscuit, ready to add butter.

She stared at him momentarily. "I was actually, but thought it rather rude to ask. Since you brought it up…" She smiled but felt like crying. All she wanted was to be held by him.

He nodded gently. "I've been standing there every morning since our last time together, hoping you'd come outside." His hand slid across the table and he covered her hand. It almost felt like he was holding it there so she couldn't take it from him.

"Oh." She wasn't sure what to say. That was a very big statement he'd made. At least in her mind it was. His words told her he'd missed Victoria every bit as much as she'd missed him. It almost made her cry.

"I've regretted our last moments together," he said. "Regretted that I didn't argue with you, and didn't fight to stay together."

He stared at their entwined hands. "I can't sleep, Victoria. Every waking moment is spent thinking of you. I have to read and re-read my recipes, sometimes throwing the mixture out because I can't concentrate and have messed it up."

She knew how he felt. The same thing was happening to her. She swallowed. "I don't know how we can fix it," she said quietly.

"I love you, Victoria. Marry me."

Her jaw dropped in the exact way her mother had told her was *extremely unladylike*. She couldn't help it, this was one of the moments when jaws had a mind of their own. "I love you too," she whispered, " But there seems no solution in this instance."

"Good morning." Mrs Baker entered the kitchen and Jesse snatched his hand away so quickly the motion almost burned her skin.

She had that look about her. The one that said *I know exactly what you two are up to and you'd better cut it out.*

Jesse looked guilty beyond redemption, and she felt just as bad. How much had Mrs Baker heard she wondered.

"I wondered how long it would take before you came calling," she said, staring at Jesse.

He seemed to slink down in his seat. "Good morning, Mrs Baker," he said in response. She didn't seem surprised.

"Ah, Victoria. You've made biscuits. How are they Mr Pendleberry?"

"Very nice, as a matter of fact," he said, then took a mouthful of his coffee.

Mrs Baker nodded thoughtfully. "Perhaps when you are married, Victoria will make them for you."

Jesse near spat his coffee out across the table.

Chapter Eight

Jesse wasn't sure where his energy suddenly came from, but he felt wide awake.

Mrs Baker's words had startled him – there was no other way to put it. Victoria gaped at the woman, then her face formed a grin.

For someone who had warned him off Victoria, this was a complete turn-about.

His business had become quite busy over the past weeks. Once word had got around town, the good citizens of Grand Falls had frequented his store.

He was absolutely certain the word of Mrs Baker and her friend Mrs Davis had a lot to do with it. Those two seemed to be quite influential around here.

Jesse was not complaining. He and Victoria were meeting at the diner later, and would discuss where to go from here. It was not everyday you got the blessing of the woman who'd originally blocked their relationship – before it even began.

He was bottling Ginger Tonic for a customer, when the bell over the door tinkled. "Good morning, Mrs Baker," he said, then glanced at his pocket-watch.

"Ah, it is afternoon. Good Afternoon to you then", he said smiling. "I'm afraid your order isn't ready yet. I'd planned for Young Mr Ambrewster to deliver it after school."

"I'm not here for that, Mr Pendleberry." She pursed her lips and waved an unsealed letter across in front of him. "This letter arrived today – I'm just back from collecting it."

He tried to read the sender but she continued to wave it about.

"The letter is from the Director of Education," she said. Her expression was grim, and he was certain it was confirmation Victoria had lost her job because of the unrelenting gossip.

"I'm sorry it's come to this," he said quietly. "Victoria loves her job, and adores her students."

"My dear Mr Pendleberry, you do not understand." She clutched the letter against her chest. "I do wish Miss Hudson was here now, since it concerns you both."

That confused him. Why would she wish Victoria to hear bad news. Despite that, he pulled his pocket-watch out again and checked the time. "It will be their lunch break in five minutes. Would you care to take a stroll to the school?"

She stared at him for what seemed forever, but finally nodded her acceptance. "Why not?" she said, and clutched the letter to her chest again.

"Why not indeed?" he asked, and guided her out the door, locking it behind him.

Mrs Baker hooked her arm through his as they made their way to the school. She said not a word, but held her head high.

Dread filled him, but Jesse didn't want Victoria to hear the news alone. They were in this together, and if she lost her job because of it, he was more than prepared to support her.

He had asked her to marry him after all.

They had yet to go and see the preacher, or make any sort of plans, but that was on the agenda for tonight. Perhaps now it would be a rather somber affair. Instead of celebrating their engagement, it seemed they would be commiserating over Victoria losing her job. A vocation she adored.

As they rounded the corner, the children came streaming out of the school carrying their lunch pails. They sat quietly on the rocks and wooden seats scattered about.

There was no sign of Victoria.

"Where's Miss Hudson," Jesse asked, feeling concerned as she usually followed them out.

Anna pointed toward the front door to the school. "She's making a mug of tea. She'll be out soon." She pulled the lid off her lunch pail and began to eat.

"Thank you, Miss Meyer," Jesse said. He always made a point of addressing young people by their proper names, believing it far more respectful.

He took a deep breath and let it out slowly. He was anxious to hear what was in the letter, but if it was bad news, as he suspected, it was better left unread.

Taking the few steps to the schoolroom felt like one hundred steps. His legs felt so heavy from the stress of it all. "Victoria," he said once they were inside. "Mrs Baker has news for us."

Victoria turned around slowly and faced them. "What is it?" she asked quietly, then moved toward them. Jesse pulled her into an embrace. It felt so good to have her in his arms again, and for just a moment he forgot about the impending dread.

Once again, Mrs Baker waved the envelope through the air. "I have received a letter from the Director of Education," she said matter of factly.

"Oh no!" Victoria was mortified and he pulled her closer. His heart thudded in his chest, but he knew no matter what, he would stand by her.

"I wrote to him some time back," Mrs Baker said, and glanced up at them. "It is my duty you know, since I am the one who has tried for some years to get a teacher for this town." She pursed her lips as if to say there will be no further discussion on the matter.

"I explained how much in love you two were, and how terrified you were, Victoria, of the students once again being left without a teacher. It was my concern too."

She glanced up from the letter and stared at them. "He totally agrees with me." She let her words trail off and stared at the pair. "The Minister has agreed to allow you to marry, and for Victoria to keep her position of schoolmarm."

Victoria looked up at Jesse as tears streamed down her face. He pulled her close and kissed her, then whispered in her ear. "Let's get married now," he said, and cradled her against him.

The plan had been to meet at the diner that night and decide their future.

Now they had the blessing of both Mrs Baker and the Minister of Education, it would be far easier. They sat opposite each other, holding hands, and staring into each other's eyes.

Victoria couldn't believe how that horrid train ride had changed her life. She wondered what she would be doing right now if Jesse hadn't sat across from her in the carriage. And how it would have all panned out if they hadn't bumped into each other again on the platform.

If he'd stayed on the train, and gone even one more station along the track, they would not be sitting opposite each other planning their marriage now. Nor would they be thinking about the rest of their lives together.

She sighed. What had she done to be so lucky as to have met Jesse Pendleberry?

Jesse glanced up at her and smiled, then patted her hand. "It is a bit like that, isn't it? I feel like we're in the middle of a fairytale. When I woke up this morning, I had no idea we would be sitting here planning our wedding. Did you?"

She shook her head. "I honestly thought I'd never see you again. I was broken-hearted at the thought of it." She swallowed hard, and tears came to her eyes. "I thought I'd lost you forever."

He lifted his hand and gently wiped her tears away. "I always hoped we'd find a way. I was not prepared to lose you, no matter what it took." He lifted her hand and kissed it. "I love you far too much to contemplate losing you."

"Oh, Jesse," she said, tears streaming down her face now. "I love you more than you'll ever know."

Mrs Baker came and stood by their table. "What's this then? I thought you'd be happy?"

Jesse pulled out a kerchief and handed it to Victoria. "Happy tears," he said. "I never did thank you, Mrs Baker for all you've done. None of this would be possible without your help."

She glanced at him and nodded. "True love always finds a way. I knew from that first moment you two were meant for each other."

She handed them each a menu. "Are you ready to order, or are you just going to sit here gazing into each other's eyes?" She grinned, and Victoria's heart soared. How could they ever thank this wonderful lady for what she'd done for them?

Without thinking, she stood and wrapped her arms around Mrs Baker, who was more like a mother to her than a friend. "Thank you," she whispered. "We wouldn't be together if it wasn't for you."

As she stepped back, the older woman wiped tears from her own eyes. "You are very welcome," she said quietly, then quickly headed for the kitchen.

That caused Victoria's tears to begin once more, and Jesse stood, wrapping his arms around her. She leaned her head against his chest and thought about the first time he'd held her. She never wanted him to let her go, and now he didn't have to.

They were about to get their forever.

Two Weeks Later...

Victoria stood outside the entrance to the church. Mrs Baker stood by her side, and had agreed to give her away. Joe Harkley, the town's tailor, had agreed to make a gown for her wedding, and had done it in record time.

The children had been ecstatic when she'd told them she was marrying Dr Pendleberry and she would still be their teacher. Johnny ran up and hugged her, he'd been so happy. "I knew it," he whispered, then grinned at her. She couldn't help but smile back at him.

Never in her wildest dreams did she imagine she'd be waiting to walk down the aisle into the arms of her soon-to-be husband. Jesse was right – it was something out of a fairytale. She'd never believed in fairytales until now.

The organ music began to play and Mrs Baker tightened her grip. "That's our cue," she said, and they began to move slowly inside.

Jesse turned to face them; he looked so handsome in his new suit Joe had made for him. His smile lit up the entire church, and her heart fluttered.

"Oh!" She hadn't noticed before, but her students stood either side of the aisle and formed a guard of honor. A stray tear trickled down her face. "What a beautiful thing to do," she whispered as they continued walking.

As they got closer, Victoria hugged each one of her students. The boys stood tall and tried to pretend it hadn't affected them, but the girls were all crying and sobbing. "I'm not going anywhere," she said gently. "School is still on next week!"

They reached the front of the church, and Preacher Devon said, "Who gives this woman away?"

"I do," Mrs Baker said, tears in her eyes. Until recently, Victoria had no idea how emotional the woman could be. She'd always presented as a person of strength, but even strong people were allowed to have their moments.

Jesse reached out and took both her hands, guiding her to stand beside him.

"Dearly Beloved," the preacher began.

When it was all over, Jesse pulled her close and kissed her. Then they began their trek down the aisle and outside. Victoria hadn't noticed how many people were there when she entered. Practically the entire town had come to witness their nuptials.

Her students beat them outside, and threw rice at them as they left. Then the rest of the congregation joined them, and she wriggled as rice slid down her back.

Victoria glanced about, taking in every person there, every face. She wanted to have that memory for all time. Today would be one of the most memorable days of her life.

Epilogue

One year later…

Victoria stood out the front of the room, teaching her students. Johnny had been an enormous help over the past year or so, and continued to be. He was doing so well, Jesse had promised him that apprenticeship, and he'd already learned a lot at the Apothecary. On his fifteenth birthday he would begin his apprenticeship. He was beyond excited.

She was so proud of him, and knew Johnny would do wonderfully. He had the passion to do it, and Jesse would make sure he studied hard once he began.

"Please pull out your workbooks, then turn to page twenty of…" She clutched at her stomach, then abruptly sat.

Johnny was instantly by her side. "Mrs Pendleberry? Are you alright?" He looked more than a little concerned.

She nodded, but he saw through her. "I'll go get Doc Pendleberry, then Doc Spencer." He gripped her hand. "You stay right here." He turned to his fellow students. "Walter, you take over the class while I'm gone." The boy agreed, and Johnny was gone.

People said she couldn't do it, but Victoria had managed to continue teaching during her confinement. She hadn't intended to work until the birth, and Jesse had tried to convince her to stop, but she'd resisted. So now here she was, her contractions coming fast and furious.

The door flung open and there he stood – her wonderful husband. He rushed toward her and held her tight. "Do you think you can walk home?" he whispered. Walter glanced back over his shoulder, but continued with the planned lesson.

"Honestly, I don't know," she whispered back, then tried to stand. "Oh no!" She looked down in despair at the puddle at her feet. "My waters just broke," she said quietly, not wanting the children to hear.

He stared at her for what seemed forever, but was only a few seconds, then scooped her up and carried her toward the door. "Someone open the door please?" he called over his shoulder, and Walter came running.

Johnny arrived about the same time. "Doc Spencer is out on a job up in the mountains. Mrs Spencer doesn't know when he'll be back." The boy looked upset, but no more than Victoria was.

"What are we going to do," she wailed, her head close to her husband's chest.

He carefully carried her down the steps. "Mr Ambrewster, please call Mrs Baker to help. I can't deliver this baby on my own."

Victoria's eyes opened wide. "You're going to deliver our baby?"

"I am a doctor, Victoria. Besides, we have no choice." He carried her all the way home and placed her on their marital bed after laying folded towels and sheets over it.

Soon after Johnny arrived with Mrs Baker. "What can I do to help, Sir?"

"I'll need my medical bag from the store. Can you fetch it please?" Johnny was back in record time. "Now put on some water to boil, then go back to the school and take over."

"Yes, Sir." He looked disappointed, and no doubt could have helped given he'd been brought up on a farm. But Victoria did not want one of her students helping to birth her baby. She'd never be able to face him again.

Jesse scrubbed his hands clean and Mrs Baker did the same. Victoria screamed.

"It's coming," she said, panting.

Mrs Baker looked skeptical. "That's far too quick, my dear. First babies usually take some hours." She glanced at Jesse and he agreed.

"Well this baby told me it was ready to come about midnight," she said, continuing to pant.

"Oh my Lord," Jesse said. "Why didn't you tell me?"

She screamed again. "Because I had lessons to deliver."

She could see he was frustrated, but why waste good hours of teaching if it could be avoided? "Arghhhhhhh!"

"I can see the head," Jesse said. "This baby really is coming." He turned to his wife. "I want you to hold Mrs Baker's hand as tight as you can, then push hard."

He glanced at her. "Can you do that?"

She nodded, then pushed. "This is all your fault, Jesse," she ground out.

"Well, I surely hope so, darlin'." He grinned at her but she didn't find it funny.

She pushed again.

"Nearly there. One more big push and you should be done."

Then a thought struck her. "Have you delivered a baby before, Jesse?"

He glanced up at her again, and then at Mrs Baker. "Come on, you can do it. One more push."

"Jesse?"

"Push!" He looked down at the tiny creature in his arms and Mrs Baker joined him.

"You have a beautiful baby girl," she said, and Victoria watched as she held back tears. "Why don't you close your eyes for just a moment, have a short rest while Dr Pendleberry does what he has to do?"

As the baby screamed, she closed her eyes momentarily, waiting to receive her in her arms. Finally she was handed over and Victoria held her tight.

"Can we call her Maisie, after my grandmother?" Victoria asked as the baby continued to scream.

"Of course, whatever you want," Jesse said gently as he continued to work.

"She's probably hungry," Mrs Baker said. "Why don't you feed her. I'll leave you two alone for a while." She quietly slipped out of the room.

Jesse joined her and the baby. "She's beautiful," he said, then kissed her gently.

"Yes, she is," Victoria said. "You never did answer. Have you delivered a baby before?"

"There's a first time for everything," he said winking at her. "I'm really pleased that it happened to be our own precious daughter."

Victoria agreed. She said a silent prayer of thanks for the miracle of her own precious family, and knew they would have more moments like this.

From the Author

Thank you for reading *Victoria!* I hope you enjoyed Victoria and Jesse's story as much as I enjoyed writing it. The *Brides of Montana* series continues with *Maggie*.

Books in this series are as follows:

Emily

Grace

Victoria

Maggie

Callie

Olivia

To find out about new books, sign up for my newsletter at:

cheryl-wright.com/newsletter/

About the Author

Multi-published, award-winning and bestselling author Cheryl Wright, former secretary, debt collector, account manager, writing coach, and shopping tour hostess, loves reading.

She writes both historical and contemporary western romance, as well as romantic suspense.

She lives in Melbourne, Australia, and is married with two adult children and has six grandchildren. When she's not writing, she can be found in her craft room making greeting cards.

Links

Website: *http://www.cheryl-wright.com/*

Facebook Reader Group:
https://www.facebook.com/groups/cherylwrightauthor/

Join My Newsletter:

https://cheryl-wright.com/newsletter/